Nicky

Also by Michelle Gordon:

Fiction:

Earth Angel Series:

The Earth Angel Training Academy

The Earth Angel Awakening

The Other Side

The Twin Flame Reunion

The Twin Flame Retreat

The Twin Flame Resurrection

The Twin Flame Reality

The Twin Flame Rebellion

The Twin Flame Reignition

The Earth Angel Revolution

Visionary Collection

Heaven dot com

The Doorway to PAM

The Elphite

I'm Here

The Onist

Duelling Poets

Non-fiction:

Where's My F**king Unicorn?

Oracle Cards:

Aria's Oracle

Velvet's Oracle

Amethyst's Oracle

Laguz's Oracle

Michelle Gordon

theamethystangel.com

First published in Great Britain in 2007 by Michelle Gordon
Second Edition published in Great Britain in 2011 by The Amethyst Angel
Third Edition Published in Great Britain in 2014 by The Amethyst Angel
Fourth Edition Published in Great Britain in 2018 by The Amethyst Angel

ISBN: 978-1-912257-30-0

Fourth Edition

This book is dedicated to my dad, for always believing in my writing, and my English teacher Miss Janine Phillips, for always reading my work, and encouraging me to keep going.

Chapter One

Christina glanced up at James, taking in every little detail of his face, his straight nose, strong jaw and the tiny dimple in his cheek. His dark hair was ruffled by the slight breeze.

James looked at Christina and smiled. The dimple deepened, making Christina smile back.

"I wish we could stay here forever." He gestured toward the sea, the sun glistening off the rippling surface.

Christina's smile faded, and she frowned. "Why do we have to leave?"

He stopped and turned to her, gently grasping her shoulders. "Chrissy, you know you can't stay here. Not yet."

Beep...beep...beep. He looked at his watch, but made no move to turn off the alarm.

"No," she whispered. "I don't want to leave. I want to stay here, with you."

Christina stared up into James' eyes, and detected a deep sadness there. Just as she was about to ask him what was wrong, the beeping became louder, more insistent, and it pierced her thoughts, making her head ache.

She rubbed her eyes. "Can't you switch that off? It's hurting me."

James wrapped his arms around her. "You know I can't do that. It's not the right time."

Christina rested her head against his shoulder. The beeping seemed to get louder still.

"When is the right time?"

James gestured at the golden disc in the sky above them.

"When the sun sets."

Beep...beep...beep.

* * *

When Christina woke up, for a split second, she felt no pain and she felt so free that she thought that maybe she had passed on to the next world. But when she opened her eyes, the sounds of the busy hospital around her became clear, the beeping monitor at her bedside became louder, the white ceiling came into focus, and her pain returned with such intensity that she let out a shallow gasp.

Struggling to breathe through the pain, Christina tried desperately not to cry, but still a tear trickled down her cheek. She longed to wipe it away, but she was just too weak to lift her hand. For the last few weeks, her family had praised her for being so brave, so optimistic despite her condition that she couldn't let them down now. Not when it seemed that the end was so close. But the truth was, she was scared. As much as she wanted rid of the pain, she just couldn't imagine not being alive. The thought of not existing hurt more than the intense physical pain she had endured for the last few weeks of her life.

Christina closed her eyes and bit her dry, chapped lip. Another tear squeezed out and made its way down her cheek, dripping onto her favourite pink nightie. She took as deep a breath as she could and let it out slowly. Then she opened her eyes and resolved not to cry another tear.

After all, when she finally left, she wanted people to remember her as being brave, not a sobbing wreck. It was a silly thing to worry about, but Christina felt that the only thing she had left to hold onto was her pride.

Christina turned her head to the side, toward the curtained window, wincing slightly at the pain it caused her. She could see the sunlight peeping around the edges of the heavy curtains. It seemed like so long since she had felt the sun on her face, its warmth soaking into her skin. Suddenly, her dream came back to her in a rush, and she smiled. If there was such a thing as an afterlife, she hoped it would be just like her dream.

* * *

A sound coming from her right made her turn her head back slowly. The door was opening, but she was lying so flat that she couldn't see who was entering the room.

"Good morning!" a cheery female voice called out. "How are we feeling today?"

A face came into Christina's vision, and she groaned inwardly. It was the ever-cheerful Nurse Williams. Throughout all the time Christina had been confined to her hospital bed, she had never seen Nurse Williams in a bad mood.

The bedside lamp was flicked on, filling the room with a dim light that created huge shadows of the plump nurse on the ceiling. Another nurse entered the room, and together they transferred Christina to a trolley while they changed the sheets on her bed. Then they gently lifted Christina back onto the bed, propping her up on a mound of pillows.

"Your visitors will be here soon," Nurse Williams said. "Do you want me to get you anything?"

"No, I'm fine," Christina mumbled.

Nurse Williams' voice softened. "Okay sweetie." She replaced the buzzer in Christina's hand. "Just press the button if you need anything. Okay?"

"Yes."

"I'll come and check on you in a little while."

Christina nodded her head slightly.

The two nurses left the room, leaving Christina to her thoughts again. It wasn't long before the door opened again. This time, Christina could see who was coming into the private room. It was James. His hair was dishevelled, his clothes rumpled and un-ironed. Christina smiled, thinking of all the mornings she'd woken up, lying next to him, and watched him sleep. His hair never behaved first thing in the morning. He smiled back gently and closed the door behind him. He came over to the bed and kissed her on the forehead, then he slipped off his jacket and laid it over the plastic chair, before sitting on the edge of her bed.

He took her pale hand in his and studied her face, he noticed her wet cheeks immediately.

"Hey," he said softly. "What is it?"

She bit her lip, willing herself not to cry. James was the only person who knew just how scared she was of dying. When she'd first been diagnosed, he'd held her in his arms while she cried. He'd comforted her and picked up her spirits when she was down. And when she couldn't be cheered up, he understood. He never once complained when she hadn't felt like doing anything but cuddling. So right now, she didn't want to burden him yet again but she also didn't want to lie to him. He deserved more than that.

"I got scared," she whispered, staring down at her white

blankets. James reached out his hand and lifted her chin gently so that she would look at him.

"I'm here now, there's nothing to be scared of," he said, his voice rough with emotion. He smoothed away her tears with his thumb; Christina wished he could smooth away her pain just as easily.

"I know." She paused, then gave a small smile. "I had a dream last night."

"Yeah? What about? Me, I hope," James said, wiggling his eyebrows suggestively.

Christina grinned. "Actually, you *were* in it, but it wasn't anything like that. It was really, well... nice."

James grimaced comically. "Nice? Ugh, I'm going to have to brush up on my dream performance by the sound of it."

Christina shook her head. "No, silly. We were walking along the beach, holding hands. The sun was shining, and the waves were crashing onto the sand."

James raised his eyebrows. "And then what happened?"

Christina rolled her eyes. "That was it. That was the whole dream."

"Oh, well, you're right. That was a nice dream. Boring, maybe, but nice." James smiled to show he was joking. "So I didn't say anything romantic? Or devastatingly witty? We just... walked?"

"Well, yeah." Christina stopped and frowned. "No, wait. We did talk. I said I wanted to stay there forever, and you said..." Christina paused and bit her lip as she remembered the words, and realised their meaning.

"Sweetie," James said, concerned, "what did I say?"

"The sunset," Christina whispered.

James frowned. "What about it?"

"It means the end of the day." She looked at him sadly.

"And I think, the end of the pain."

James' eyes widened. Then he shook his head. "It was just a dream, Chrissy. It doesn't mean anything."

Christina wanted to argue, but she felt drained from their conversation already. An idea formed in her mind. "Well, whether it's true or not, could you do something for me?"

James took a deep breath. "Anything," he whispered.

"Make my dream come true."

"Your dream? You want to go to the beach?"

Christina nodded.

James shook his head. "I can't. It's March and it's freezing out there. The doctors would never let me take you out of hospital. Not at this stage." He stared at the floor.

"I don't care," Christina said stubbornly. "You could say I wanted some fresh air or something, then when we're outside, you could just get me in the car and -"

"Chrissy, I can't. I just can't," James interrupted.

"Why not?"

James lifted his gaze to hers. "Because if anything happened to you," his voice broke, "then I'd never forgive myself."

"Well," Christina said slowly, "if you don't come and take me to the beach, take me away from here, then," she looked him straight in the eye. "I'll never forgive you."

James gasped. Hurt was written plainly across his face, but Chrissy didn't look away. It pained her to say something so cruel to the person she loved most in the world, but it was the only way she could make him see how important this was to her.

James let go of her hand, got up and walked over to the window.

Christina squeezed her eyes shut and tried not to cry. She knew that James would rather die than hurt her and that was why he was hesitant to take her away from the hospital. It wasn't because he didn't want to grant her wish.

"James?"

James turned his head toward the bed, not meeting her gaze.

"The basic fact is, whether I'm in here, on the beach or on the moon, I'm going to die. And that scares me so much." Her voice shook, and she struggled to catch her breath. "But I just know, that if I was with you, in my favourite place, then it wouldn't seem so scary." Tired, Christina slumped back into the pillows, her eyes closed.

Silence blanketed the room. Christina took a deep breath and opened her eyes. A sliver of sunlight was peeping through the middle of the curtains, shining onto James' face, making his tears glisten. She bit her lip. She didn't want to fight. Not so close to the end. She was just about to say that if he couldn't do it, then it was okay, when James broke the silence.

"Okay," he whispered, so quietly Christina could barely hear him. He took a deep breath then walked back to her bed. He sat on the side again and took her hand, stroking it gently. "I'll do it." He met her gaze and smiled weakly at her. "You know I could never say no to you."

Christine wrapped her fingers around his and squeezed them as tightly as she could.

"Thank you." She smiled at him, her first real smile since that morning when she woke up knowing that today would be the last day of her life.

They sat in a comfortable silence for a while, just enjoying each other's company. They used to spend ages just sitting together, not having to speak a word, knowing exactly what the other was thinking.

Suddenly, Christina remembered she had something

important to ask.

"Did you manage to set up the account?"

James sighed, as though he had hoped she'd forgotten. "Yes. The account is set up and the letters are typed and ready to go."

"Were you able to use the address I thought up?"

"Of course. I did everything exactly the way you wanted it."

Christina smiled. "Thank you," she whispered. "It means so much to me."

James leaned over and kissed her on the forehead, then on her cracked lips. "I know."

They sat silently for a while, both lost in their thoughts.

"James?"

He smiled at her, and brushed a strand of hair from her face. "Yes?"

"Hold me?"

James nodded, a tear escaping down his cheek. Slowly, he leaned forward and put his arms around her, holding her as tightly as he could without hurting her. She rested her head on his shoulder.

"I love you, James."

"I love you too, Angel."

After a while, James noticed that Christina's breathing had become deep and even, and he realised she had fallen asleep. James carefully disentangled himself from her and laid her back against the pillows. His heart ached at seeing her so pale, so fragile. He kissed her lightly on the forehead, then stood and picked up his jacket.

"See you later, Angel."

Chapter Two

A while later, Christina woke up to find her parents and brother sitting around her bedside, just watching her. She hid the wave of intense pain that washed over her with a weak smile.

"Hey Mum, Dad, Adam," she said, her voice thick with sleep. "How long have you been here? You should have woken me."

Her mother, who was sitting closest to her, stroked Christina's hand. "We haven't been here too long, honey. You looked so peaceful, we didn't want to wake you up." A tear hung on the edge of her dark eyelashes. She blinked and it fell down her cheek. "How are you feeling?"

Christina shrugged slightly. "The same."

For a moment, they all just sat quietly, watching her. Christina couldn't stand the silence any longer.

"So, what's been happening out there in the real world?"

"Well," her mother said slowly, struggling to think of something to say, "Oh! I bumped into Mrs Jones, your old piano teacher, she was asking about you." She thought for a moment. "Adam checked your e-mail, and he printed a couple out for you."

"Who are they from?" Christina asked.

Adam took some folded up papers out of his pocket and looked through them. "One from Joe, one from Rebecca and one from Peter." He looked up at Christina. "Would you like me to read them to you?"

Christina glanced at her parents then looked back at Adam.

"In a minute?"

"Sure."

Christina's dad saw the look on her face and took the hint. "Well, honey, we're going to get some coffee from the canteen," he said, taking his wife by the hand. "We'll be back in a little while okay?"

Christina smiled gratefully.

They left the room and Adam smiled at Christina. "Which one should I read first?"

"Peter's."

Adam rifled through the pages and picked one out. He straightened the paper, and cleared his throat.

"'Chrissy,'" Adam began. "'Your brother told me that you are unable to get to a computer right now because you've gone into hospital for treatment, but he said he'd print this out for you to read.'"

"Treatment?" Christina interrupted. "He doesn't know it didn't work?"

Adam looked up at Christina sadly. "No he doesn't. I couldn't tell him, Chrissy."

"So Peter thinks I might get better?"

Adam sighed. "Yes, he does."

"Oh." Christina bit her lip. She nodded at the e-mail in Adam's hands. "Carry on."

Adam nodded and continued reading. "'Why didn't you tell me that the cancer was worse and you had to go into hospital? You don't have to hide anything from me, Chrissy,

I'm here for you. You can tell me anything. I think of you all the time. Remember when we met? That day was amazing, and I'll never forget it. I can't wait until you start getting better and we can meet up again. Maybe we could even go out one night to look for shooting stars to wish upon. If I see one before that, I'll make a wish for you, Chrissy. I'll wish for extra strength for you to be able to beat this thing. I'll wish for your health and happiness. Meanwhile, I'm sending some 'get well' vibes with this e-mail, so I hope they help. Please ask Adam to reply to this if you can't get to a computer any time soon. Lots of love, Peter.'" Adam finished reading, and sighed. "Do you want me tell him?"

Christina used all of her strength to lift her hand to his face and stroke his cheek. "There's no need, he'll know soon."

Adam frowned. "What do you mean by that?"

Her hand fell to the bed, her strength gone. She bit her lip and looked down at the sheets.

"It's time, Adam. I've asked James to take me to the beach, tonight." She looked up at him. "This is it. Just remember how much I love you, okay?" Her voice caught on the last few words.

Adam's eyes widened as he took in the meaning of her words.

"Please don't tell Mum and Dad. They won't understand. I just want to see the sunset." She smiled longingly. "To feel the sand on my feet and the sun on my face."

Adam nodded, a lone tear falling down his cheek. He didn't trust himself to speak.

"Thank you," Christina whispered.

He took her hand in his and squeezed it gently, his tears splashing onto her pale fingers.

Just then, her parents came back into the room. They

stayed for an hour or so, promising to come in earlier the next day. Her parents hugged her, then Adam also gave her a hug. Christina could see he was struggling to keep his composure. Just as her parents were leaving the room, she called out.

"Mum, Dad?"

They turned around. "What, honey?" her mother asked.

"I love you."

Her mum and dad smiled. "We love you too," her father said. "See you tomorrow."

Christina smiled sadly.

Adam was the last to exit. He turned and ran back to give her one last hug, whispering "I love you" in her ear.

"Me, too."

He nodded and left quickly without looking back.

* * *

About an hour later, the door opened and Christina expected to see the nurse, but instead, her best friend Melanie, poked her head around the door.

Christina smiled warmly. "Mel," she whispered.

Melanie sat on the plastic chair next to the bed. She was furiously chewing on her bottom lip. Christina knew she did this when she was on the verge of tears. They'd been best friends for more than ten years, and she knew it must hurt Melanie so much to see her like this.

"Hey, Chris," Melanie said softly, taking her hand.

Christina smiled. "Wasn't expecting to see you today."

A tear escaped, and ran down Melanie's cheek. "Your brother called me," she said hoarsely.

"Oh," she said quietly.

"Oh, Chris! I don't want you to go!" Melanie burst out.

She buried her head in Christina's blankets and sobbed.

"I don't want to leave you, Mel," Christina replied, slowly and deliberately. "But I have to. You knew that ages ago."

Melanie lifted her head, and attempted to wipe away her tears. "I know," she whispered. "I'm sorry, I shouldn't act like this. After all, I'm not the one who's.... I just can't stand the thought of you not being here anymore. That we won't be able to talk on the phone, or e-mail, or go camping in the summer..." her voice trailed off as she realised how upset she was making Christina. "Oh, Chris! I'm so sorry, I didn't mean to..." She grabbed a tissue from the bedside table and gently wiped away Christina's tears. "Maybe I should go now," she said. "I keep saying the wrong thing. I didn't mean to upset you and remind you of all that..."

Christina shook her head. "No," she said. "Please don't go. I like to remember what we used to do."

Melanie frowned. "Are you sure?"

Christina smiled. "Yes."

"Do you want me to talk about what we did when we were kids?" she asked timidly.

"Please," Christina whispered.

"Okay," Melanie said, wiping away her own tears. She thought hard for a minute then smiled. "Do you remember when we were six, and we thought it would be funny to..."

* * *

Melanie stayed for about half an hour, talking about the adventures they'd had as kids. She left when she realised that Christina had fallen asleep. She kissed her best friend on the forehead.

"You'll always be my best friend, Chris. I love you." She took her hand from Christina's and quietly left the room.

She walked slowly through the corridors, tears streaming steadily down her face. In her car, she had to wait for a while before she could see well enough to make the drive home.

* * *

A short while later, a nurse came in to check on Christina. At the sound of the door opening, Christina woke up. She realised that Melanie had gone.

"What time is it?" she asked.

"It's half five, dear. Is there anything I can get you?"

Christina shook her head. "Is Nurse Williams still here?"

"No, she went home. She was on the early shift."

"Oh, I see," Christina murmured. "Never mind."

"Anything else I can do for you, honey?"

"Yes, there is. Could you open the curtains please?"

The nurse looked uncertain. "Are you sure dear? It's still quite bright outside, won't it hurt your eyes?"

Christina shrugged. "I want to see outside."

The nurse reluctantly went to the window, and slowly opened the curtains. Christina squinted as the late afternoon sun shone into the room.

The nurse turned to her. "Is that okay?"

Christina smiled. "Could you do just one more thing?"

"What's that, dear?"

"Could you move my bed over to the window? And ... and raise it up so I can look at the view?" Christina's voice was fading, and the nurse had to move closer to hear her. She patted Christina's hand.

"Okay, I'll just get another nurse to help me move all the machines. I'll be back in a minute." She left the room, and Christina continued to stare out of the window.

Minutes later, Christina was right in front of the window, staring down at the houses below. Being on the third floor, she had quite a good view of the town. The sun was getting lower in the sky. Christina bit her cracked lip.

"Hurry, James," she whispered. "Please."

* * *

Miles away, James cursed as he sat in his stationary car. The traffic on the motorway had come to a standstill. He drummed his fingers on the gearstick impatiently. Of all the nights for there to be a traffic jam, why did there have to be one tonight? He couldn't believe his bad luck. He glanced at the clock, the sun had almost set, he was too late. He punched the steering wheel. The horn sounded.

"Damn! Damn! Damn!" he yelled.

* * *

Sitting on a rock on the beach, Adam stared silently out to sea. The wind whipped through his flimsy jacket, but he didn't even notice. The sunlight glittered and danced on the turbulent sea. As the waves crashed onto the sandy shore below him, one by one, the tears he had held in when he was with Christina, fell.

"Chrissy," he whispered to the falling sun. "I won't forget you."

* * *

At her dressing table, Melanie sat, staring into her mirror. A sad, red, puffy face stared back at her. In her hands she held a framed photo. It was of herself and Christina. Adam had taken it, when the three of them had gone camping in the woods a few years back. She loved the photo, and it brought back so many sweet memories. But it hurt Melanie to think they would never go camping again, that they'd never laugh together again, that Christina just wouldn't be there anymore. Unable to bear it any longer, Melanie buried her head in her arms and let out her tears.

"Oh, Chris!" she sobbed. "I'm going to miss you so much."

* * *

A few hundred miles away, Peter lay on his bed, the sky outside his window getting darker. He thought of Chrissy. He'd only known her a short time. They'd met in a chat room on the internet. After eighteen months of e-mails and phone calls, they finally met. Sometime during those short few hours they were together, Peter fell in love with her. Not only was she beautiful, she was intelligent and sweet too. But he never told her exactly how he felt. Then she had been diagnosed with cancer. Peter sighed. At least she was being treated and was getting better. He couldn't wait to see her again. Although she had a steady boyfriend, Peter loved her, and he knew they would remain friends forever, if nothing else. He got up and went to the window. The sun had set just moments before, and the sky was all different shades of pink and purple.

"Get well soon, Chrissy."

* * *

Lying by the window, Christina watched peacefully as the sun set. She knew in her heart that James wasn't coming to take her to the beach. She knew that he would arrive too late. But she wasn't mad at him. She just hoped that nothing bad had happened to him. She felt herself getting weaker. She felt that if she closed her eyes for more than a second, she would fall asleep forever.

Christina swallowed painfully. Then just as the last of the sun fell behind the horizon, she whispered:

"I'll always be your angel, James, always."

A tear trickled down her cheek.

She closed her eyes.

* * *

Beeeeeeeeeeeeeeeeeeeeeeeeeeeeeeeeeep.

James hit his head against the steering wheel and held it there, the horn sounding one long beep. He knew he was too late. He could feel in his heart.

"NO!" he screamed. "Chrissy!"

Suddenly, the traffic started to move and he sped toward the hospital. He parked hastily, jumped out of his car and ran to the entrance. The lift doors had just closed so he sprinted up the three flights of stairs. When he got to the corridor where Christina's room was, he could already hear the continuous beep. He burst through the door, momentarily disorientated when he realised that the bed was next to the window. He rushed to her bedside and grabbed a cold hand.

Her face was white, but peaceful.

"No," he sobbed. He sat on the bed and held her to him, rocking back and forth.

He held her for a long time. Someone switched the monitor off, but the haunting sound still echoed in his mind.

After a while, he heard people enter the room. He lifted his head and saw Christina's parents, her brother and her best friend.

Tears pouring down his cheeks, he whispered, "I was too late."

Sobs wracked Mrs Butler's body, and she slumped against her husband, who couldn't stop his own tears from falling. Melanie's shoulders shook and her tears dripped onto the front of her jumper. Adam put his arm around her and held her tight.

James held Christina to him for a few minutes longer. Then he kissed her forehead, and lay her down gently on the bed. He stroked her hair out of her face, for the last time.

Christina's parents, Adam and Melanie came to stand by the bed. Mr Butler put his arm around James.

They stood there silently for what seemed like an eternity. Finally, each of them said their goodbyes to Christina, then left the room, leaving James to be on his own with her.

James sat with Christina for a while longer. He stared at her face, trying to commit every little detail to memory.

He sighed deeply, and wiped his cheeks with the back of his hand.

James kissed her pale lips softly. A lone tear fell onto her forehead.

"Sleep, my Angel," he whispered. "Sleep."

Chapter Three

It was two hours before Christina Angela Butler's funeral, and James was sitting in front of his computer in his flat. He read, then reread the words on the screen in front of him. They were Christina's words. Christina, whom he missed so very much. The screen blurred as yet more tears fell. He couldn't seem to stop them over the last few days. He wiped them away and tried to concentrate on what he was doing. It had been one of Christina's last wishes, and he was determined to make this one come true. A week before she died, she had dictated letters to him, for her friends and family: to Adam, Melanie, and Peter. Then she asked him to set up an e-mail account using the e-mail address 'angel@heaven.com'. From this address, he was to send her letters to those people. At first, James thought the idea was weird, if not a little sick. But all Christina wanted to do was settle the minds of the people closest to her, through e-mails which said she was okay and happy where she was now.

So, James had already typed up the letters, and decided that the best time to send them would be just before the funeral, so that they would receive them after they'd buried Christina. That done, James logged off and shut down his computer. He sat on his bed, and tried to compose himself.

* * *

In silence, all who had come to pay their respects sat in the huge church, and listened to Christina's favourite song, 'Anyway, Angel'. James sat next to her weeping family, and he cried silently as he remembered how he'd met Christina. It was at a gig where a local rock band called etcha were playing. While etcha were playing this song, he'd seen her on the dance floor, dancing with some friends. He had known in that instant that he had to meet her. Later in the night he'd struck up a conversation with her, and they spent the rest of the evening in the corner, talking. As they were leaving, he bought etcha's CD, wrote his phone number on it, and gave it to her. The very next day, she rang him, and they arranged to meet. Later, after they had been seeing each other for a while, she'd admitted that she used to put the song on continuous play for hours, just because it reminded her of him.

James glanced over at Christina's dad. His eyes were closed, tears streaming down his face. He, too, was probably remembering how his daughter played the song over and over again. His knuckles were white as he clenched his fist in his lap.

James looked at Adam. He sat there, looking straight ahead at the casket covered in flowers, a crumpled piece of paper in his hand. Christina's mother was sobbing, and could be heard over the beat of the music.

When the song finished, the vicar stood at the altar and said a prayer. Then he invited friends and family to stand and say something about Christina, if they wished. James looked around behind him at all of the people sat in the church. It was full, and some had come from all over the country to say goodbye.

The first one to stand up was Melanie. Slowly, she walked up to the front. James smiled encouragingly at her as she passed him.

"I'm Melanie," she whispered into the microphone. "I was Christina's best friend. We'd been friends since we were five years old. We did everything together, we were inseparable, our mothers used to joke that we were Siamese twins." She gave a small smile. "Christina was everything to me, she cheered me up when I was down, she helped me, laughed with me and loved me, just like best friends should. I just hope that wherever she is now, she's at peace."

After Melanie had returned to her seat, Adam stood, and made his way to the front, the piece of paper clutched in his hand.

"Christina was not only my sister, but she was my friend. For hours, we'd talk. About life, love, films, music - anything that came to mind. It used to drive our parents crazy when we stayed up 'til the early hours of the morning, just talking." He looked up at everyone, and tears rolled down his cheeks, hitting the stand. "I'm not very good at writing, but I wrote a poem. For Christina, my sister." He smoothed out the paper in front of him, and began to read:

"The hours we shared,
The dreams we had,
The happiness that kept us laughing,
And the times you were there for me,
Are gone now.
You are gone now.
But I'll remember those hours,
I'll still have those dreams,

And I promise I'll try to laugh.
But more than anything,
I'm still here for you."

Adam finished the poem, which had brought many more tears to the eyes of those in the pews. He went back to his seat and sat down.

James thought no one else was going to step forward, when he heard footsteps behind him. He turned slightly. It was a man, who looked like he was in his late twenties. James didn't recognise him.

The man stood in the front. "I'm Peter," he said, in a deep, sad voice. "I knew Christina through the internet." Suddenly, James knew who he was. It was one of the people that Christina had written her last e-mails to. Her internet 'boyfriend' she had joked to him.

"We'd been talking for a year and a half before we decided to meet, and when we did, I was struck by her intelligence, her beauty, her wit. After that, I knew she was ill, but I never realised how bad it was. The main reason I'm here today, is to say goodbye, as I never got to say it to her in person. I know I didn't know her as well as many of you did, but I loved Christina. She was one of a kind. I know I'll never forget her."

James closed his eyes, and more tears threatened to fall. Although he was touched by Peter's words, he felt hurt that Christina had never told him that Peter felt so strongly about her. But he couldn't blame Peter for feeling that way, not when he knew how wonderful Christina was. Who could blame any guy for falling in love with her?

* * *

A drizzle fell on the mourners as they stood around the open grave in the cold cemetery. Muffled sobs could be heard over the blustery wind. Surrounded by Christina's relatives, James held a single white rose, her favourite flower. When the vicar had finished the prayers, some people put things on top of the casket. Adam put his poem, Melanie put a soft toy, and Christina's parents put a picture of their daughter. In the end, James was alone by the grave. He kissed the rose and placed it onto the casket.

"Please understand why I didn't say anything in church, Christina. I did everything that you asked of me, except for that one last thing, and I'm sorry. I really am." He wiped his tears away with the back of his hand. "I just hope you can forgive me."

He took a step back, and stuffed his hands into the pockets of his black overcoat.

"Goodbye, Angel," he said softly. Then he walked slowly back to his car.

* * *

The muted tones of conversation ran through the house, and soft music played in the background. Mr and Mrs Butler were hosting a small get-together after the funeral. James wandered around, meeting many people who had known Christina. While getting himself a drink, he saw Peter sitting alone in the corner of the dining room. Glass in hand, James went over to him and held out his hand.

"Hey, I'm James."

Peter looked up, his eyes swollen and red. He shook James' hand. "Peter," he replied.

James sat down next to him. "That was a nice speech you gave in church."

Peter smiled. "Thanks. I wasn't sure if I should've said anything, but I just wanted everyone to know how much I'm going to miss her."

James' throat tightened. He willed himself to relax. "Yeah," he mumbled.

"I just can't believe she's gone," Peter continued. "I only met her once, but she was amazing. She radiated this warmth which made you just want to wrap your arms around her. I wish I'd got to know her better. I thought she was going to recover. I thought that we could meet up and go stargazing. We'd always talked about it you see." Peter paused and looked at James, who was having trouble keeping his anger under control.

"I loved her, I really did," Peter said sadly.

Suddenly James could restrain himself no longer. He slammed his glass on the table, stood up, knocking his chair over, and grabbed the front of Peter's shirt.

"How dare you say that!" he growled.

Peter looked stunned. "Hey, hey, what's wrong? What did I say? Calm down."

A wild look came into James' eyes and suddenly he brought back his fist and slammed it into Peter's chin. Peter hurtled backwards, moaning as his body slammed into the dining table.

"Calm down? CALM DOWN?! That's my girlfriend you're talking about! I loved her! You didn't even know her!"

Realisation dawned in Peter's eyes. "Oh God, James, I didn't realise. I'm so sorry, of course you loved her, I would never have done anything to take her away from you, I swear."

By now, a small crowd of people had gathered around them. Mr Butler intervened.

"Guys, this is Christina's funeral, please don't argue over her," he said quietly. He pulled James off Peter. James crumpled into Mr Butler's arms. Peter rubbed his chin.

"I'm sorry," James mumbled. He straightened up, then turned to Peter. "Hey, I'm sorry, okay?" Without looking at anyone, he left the room.

* * *

Later on, Peter found James sitting outside on the patio, puffing vigorously on a cigarette. He sat next to him.

"I'm really sorry about earlier. I didn't realise you were her boyfriend. She loved you very much, and you're right, I barely knew her, really..." Peter sighed deeply. "I'm sorry."

James said nothing. He held up his cigarette. "I gave these things up. Christina used to smoke too, but her parents didn't know. We gave up together. Now..." he trailed off, and took another drag of smoke.

They sat in reflective silence for a few minutes.

"Can I ask you something?" Peter asked quietly, not wanting to get into another fight, his jaw was aching.

James sighed, and took another drag. "What?" he asked.

"Why didn't you say something, in church I mean, about Christina?"

James stared at the grass growing in-between the patio slabs. He sighed again and cleared his throat. "I didn't have anything to say. I wanted to say goodbye to Christina, not to a bunch of people who knew her, but I missed my chance. She was gone before I could reach her."

Peter frowned. "I don't understand."

"She knew she was going to die that night, because she told me. I was going to take her to the beach, so she could see the sunset before she died, but I got caught up in a damn traffic jam and by the time I got to the hospital, she'd already gone."

A tear slid down Peter's cheek. "I'm so sorry, that must have hurt."

"Yeah it did." James looked at his cigarette in disgust, then dropped it onto the patio, grinding it out beneath his heel.

"Look," James said after a moment of silence. "I'm sure you're a really nice bloke, well you'd have to be, Christina loved talking to you, but I just need to be on my own for a while, okay?" With that he got up, walked around the side of the house, through the gate and down the street.

Peter watched him go and sighed. For a few minutes, he just sat there, in Christina's garden, before he clumsily wiped away his tears and went back inside.

* * *

The dark shadows of trees rushed by as the train surged forward. Peter sat quietly, staring out at the black landscape. He leaned back in his seat and closed his eyes. It was all still too unbelievable. In his mind he could see the casket, the grave, and all the crying, mourning relatives, but he still couldn't believe it. When he received the phone call from Adam, he didn't believe him. Peter had to get him to repeat it twice before it finally sunk in.

"Oh, Christina," he whispered. "Why did you have to leave? We never even watched the stars together." A tear slid down his cheek. Ever since the first e-mail, they had talked about stargazing, as they both loved to study constellations. Peter really had hoped it would happen one day.

Peter had wished so many times that he lived closer to Christina, then maybe, just maybe, they would have got together. But time went by and Christina met James. She was so happy then. Peter remembered the pang he felt when she e-mailed him to tell him all about James. As much as he was happy that she was happy, he couldn't help feeling jealous of James. Not that he ever told Christina that.

Lost deep in his thoughts, the next two hours of his journey flew by, and he was soon getting off the train. It had been a long day. He had awoken at five o'clock that morning to get to the funeral on time. He had to be in work the next day, otherwise he might have stayed there a bit longer.

Outside his front door, he paid the taxi driver, then warily stumbled up the steps to his flat. Once inside, he didn't bother with the main light, but flicked on his bedside lamp instead. It was now nearly midnight and all Peter wanted to do was fall into bed. But then he remembered that he had to check his e-mail before work the next day, as he was expecting some important documents. Sighing, Peter picked up his laptop from his desk and settled onto his bed. He switched on the computer and logged onto the internet, then went straight to his e-mail account. He stared at the screen, trying desperately to keep his eyes open.

"*Ting*! You've got mail," the voice on his computer said. Peter opened his inbox and saw that he had three e-mails. One was a junk mail, one was from an address he did not recognise, and the last one was from work. He deleted the junk mail then opened the one from work. He read through it, then made a mental note to reply when he got to work the next morning. He was just about to log off when he remembered the other e-mail. He opened it quickly, and almost fainted from shock when he read the first few lines. He scanned through it, then read it through a second time, this time carefully. He could not believe his eyes.

“Dear Peter,

I know that this e-mail will come as a shock to you, and I also know that being the sceptical guy that you are, you’ll probably think this is a joke, but I promise you, it’s not. It’s me, Christina. I just wanted you to know that I’m fine. I know you are sad that you didn’t get the chance to say goodbye, and I’m sorry for not telling you how bad my illness was. But I’m happy now. I’m in this amazing place where there is so much love and light, I know on earth we would say that it’s heaven, but it’s even better than that!

Peter, I want you to promise that you will never be sad about me. That you’ll look back at our e-mails and remember how we made each other laugh, and how in that one time that we met, we became such good friends. I know that you wished we could have been more than that, but I hope you realise just how much I valued our friendship.

I’ll miss you, Peter, you’re a great guy who’s going to have a long and wonderful life.

Love, Christina.

P.S. Watch the stars, Peter, and I’ll be there, looking down on you, always.

By the time he had read the e-mail a fifth time, the tears were flowing freely down Peter’s cheeks. He looked at the e-mail address the letter had been sent from and smiled: angel@heaven.com.

“Oh, Chrissy, I will, I really will,” he whispered. Then he logged off the internet, shut down his laptop, and fell asleep on top of his covers.

* * *

Bee-bee-bee-beep. Bee-bee-bee-beep. Bee-bee-bee-beep.

Drowsily, Peter reached out to hit the snooze button on his alarm, but instead he knocked the clock off his nightstand and it hit the floor. Still it continued beeping.

Groaning, Peter hauled himself out of bed. Then he picked up the clock and finally switched off the alarm. He looked at the time and swore.

"Why do I do this every damn morning?" he muttered to himself as ran around his flat, dressing, brushing his teeth and drinking coffee at the same time. Ten minutes later, he grabbed his wallet, mobile, and laptop, then was out of the door and jumping in his car to go to work.

When he arrived, he rushed into the office making apologies to anyone who was listening. No one was. Hot and bothered, Peter slumped down into his chair and tried to get his breath. He was just getting out his laptop when he suddenly remembered the e-mail.

Peter frowned to himself. "Was I just dreaming?" he muttered.

"What was that, Peter?" His colleague, Mitchell leaned over to Peter's desk.

Peter shook his head. Typical. They listened to him when he didn't want them to, and they were as deaf as posts when he wanted them to listen.

"Uh, nothing, Mitch," he said, forcing a smile. "Just talking to myself, you know."

Mitchell nodded his head seriously. "Yeah, I do it all the time mate. It's okay, you don't have to explain." With that, he turned back to his own computer.

Peter shook his head in amazement. How Mitchell had even got the job in the first place was a mystery to him. He was by far the thickest person Peter had ever met. Sighing, Peter plugged in his laptop and switched it on.

"It's still here," Peter whispered, reading the e-mail. "It wasn't a dream." He swallowed, trying to keep the tears back. He didn't know what to do. Suddenly, it came to him. "Melanie," he said a little louder. He took his wallet from his pocket, and found the scrap of paper with Melanie's e-mail address on it. Quickly, he typed her an e-mail, asking her if she knew anything about it all, and if she'd received an e-mail from Christina. He sent it, then tried to get on with some work.

Chapter Four

"Mum, I'm fine, honestly. I just need to be alone." Melanie said, closing her bedroom door. She leaned against the back of the door and sighed. Even after all the tears she had shed, another one managed to crawl down her cheek. After the funeral the day before, Melanie had been thinking of Christina constantly. She couldn't concentrate on anything else. She couldn't bring herself to eat and she couldn't even think about work. Nothing seemed to interest her at all. Although she was glad to have seen and talked to Christina the day she died, she just wished she knew if Christina had heard her when she had said goodbye. She sat on her bed and sighed. She needed something to distract her for a while. She looked around her bedroom and her gaze came to rest on her computer. She went to her desk and decided to catch up on her e-mails, maybe even chat in an online chatroom. She hadn't been on the internet for a long time, as she had had too much to think about. She switched the computer on, then logged onto the net.

"Bing!" the computer sounded. Written in the box was: 'You have six new messages.' Melanie opened her inbox. There were three from her American e-mail friend, which she read and replied to. There were two junk mails and one from 'p_f_w_2000@hotmail.com'. She opened it. It was from Peter. She read in amazement about the e-mail he'd received from Christina.

"Wow," she whispered to the screen. "Are you kidding me?" Then a pang of sadness hit her. Peter had received one, but she hadn't. Her chest tightened, and she thought she was going to cry again. She didn't answer Peter's e-mail. Before deleting them, she opened the junk mail. The first one was a competition to win a holiday in Barbados. She deleted it. The second one had a weird e-mail address. Melanie opened it, then gasped in shock and happiness when she read the first few lines.

"Dear Melanie,

Being the superstitious girl that you are, I know that you will believe that this e-mail is from me, your best friend, Chris. I know I don't need to convince you, but just in case you have doubts, it was you who ate that chocolate cake when we were seven, not Molly the dog!

I really hope that you're okay, because I am. I'm at peace, healthy and happy. And I want you to be all those things too. It really is amazing here, you are literally bathed in love and everyone helps, loves and cares about each other. It's brilliant, I really wish you could see it. But you'll just have to wait I suppose!!

Really though, I'm okay, and I haven't forgotten you or any other of my friends. I love you Melanie, and although far apart, we're still the Siamese twins we always were!

Love for eternity,
Chris.

P.S. You'll always be my best friend, Mel, I love you."

Melanie smiled through the tears that coursed down her cheeks. For the first time in weeks, Melanie was really happy. So happy in fact, that the smile turned into laughter.

"Oh, Chris," she murmured. "I love you too, girl!"

* * *

Melanie answered Peter's e-mail, saying that she had received one too, and she knew it was definitely from Christina. Later that week, Melanie was walking aimlessly around town when she spotted Adam, looking in the window of a jewellers. She came up behind him.

"Hey," she said softly, placing her hand on his shoulder. He turned around and smiled slightly.

"Hi, Melanie," he said quietly, turning back to the window.

She stood next to him. "What are you looking for?" she asked.

He shook his head. "You'll just think I'm being stupid."

Melanie sighed. "Of course I won't think that. What is it?"

He pointed to a ring in the display. It was a delicate silver band with an amethyst stone set in the middle.

"I promised her. I promised I'd buy it for her birthday."

"I'm sorry," Melanie whispered.

"I just miss her so much," he whispered, his gaze set on the ring.

"I know," she said softly. "I miss her too." She put her arm around him. He turned to her and smiled gratefully.

"Do you want to go get some coffee?" Melanie asked.

Adam nodded, then with one last look at the ring, they walked down the street to the coffee shop.

* * *

"I just can't get over it, Mel," Adam said over the rim of his coffee cup. "I wake up in the morning, and for a moment, just a moment, I forget that she's gone. Then I remember everything, and I just want to go back to sleep and never wake up." He put his cup back on the table.

Melanie covered his hand with hers. "I know what you mean, Adam. Just the other day I picked up the phone and I was halfway through dialling her number when it hit me that she wouldn't be there."

"You should have rung anyway, we could have talked." Adam said.

"How long are you staying with your parents?"

Adam sighed. "Just for another week. Then I have to go back to the City." He raked a hand through his hair. "I've missed so much work, visiting Chrissy and everything, but my boss has been really great."

Melanie smiled. "That's good."

Adam smiled back distractedly. "Yeah it is, I guess."

Melanie frowned. "Don't you like working there?"

"I don't know," Adam said, shrugging, "sometimes I just..."

"Just what?" Melanie prompted.

Adam thought for a minute then shook his head. "Never mind."

Silence fell between them.

Melanie stirred her hot chocolate thoughtfully. "Have you been on the internet lately?"

Adam grimaced. "The internet? I haven't even thought about it, why?"

Melanie shrugged. "Just thought you might want to

check your e-mail that's all."

Adam frowned, confused. "What are you talking about?"

"Just humour me, okay? Check it when you get home."

"Okay, I will." Adam looked at his watch. "Speaking of home, I better get going. I promised Mum I wouldn't be long. She's at home on her own." He stood up, and put his coat on. "I'll call you sometime okay?"

Melanie nodded, and he left the coffee shop, hunching his shoulders against the cold winds outside.

* * *

"Mum, I'm home!" Adam called out as he entered his parents' house. He hung up his coat then paused. He could hear loud music coming from the lounge. He walked through the house, and was blasted by the noise as he opened the lounge door. He almost passed out at the sight that greeted him.

"Mum!" he shouted. He ran to the CD player and stopped the CD in the middle of 'Anyway, Angel'. Then he rushed to his mother and knelt by her side. She was lying on the floor, surrounded by photos of Christina, and tablets. Adam shook her gently. "Mum," he said loudly. "Mum, can you hear me? How many have you taken? Mum! Can you hear me?" He jumped up and grabbed the phone, dialling 999, while he continued to hold his mother's hand, shaking her, trying desperately to wake her up.

"I need an ambulance," he said to the operator. He told her the details, the address, and she told him to put his mother into the recovery position, then wait for the ambulance. He hung up. When he turned his mother onto her side, he saw the tablet bottle. He snatched it up. "Paracetamol," he murmured. Judging from the empty bottle and only a few tablets scattered on the floor, Adam guessed that she must have taken quite a lot. He stared at his mother's pale face. "Why, Mum? Why would you do this?"

Five minutes later, he heard a siren in the distance. The ride to the hospital was the longest one of his life. He held his mother's hand, and prayed to God - to anyone who would listen - that his mother would be okay.

* * *

The plastic chairs were cold and uncomfortable, and Adam was constantly shifting around in his seat. His eyes darted around, taking in the details of the sterile corridor in which he sat. He hated this hospital. It reminded him of the times Chrissy had spent in there, with tubes running through her weak body. Adam closed his eyes, but still, a tear managed to squeeze out. The pain of losing Chrissy was still fresh.

"Mum," he whispered, "don't you dare leave me. Not now."

Just then, a doctor came out into the hall. Adam wiped his face and jumped up. "How is she?" he asked quickly, searching the doctor's face.

The doctor stared at the floor for a second before he met Adam's eyes. "I'm sorry, Adam, it doesn't look good."

Adam's heart plummeted and he collapsed back into the plastic chair. "What?" he whispered. He shook his head. "No, please, no."

"We pumped her stomach, but some of the pills had already entered her blood stream, poisoning her. Tonight is crucial."

Adam closed his eyes, breathed deeply and tried to stop the tears, but it was futile. Head in hands, he sobbed helplessly.

* * *

Night fell, and Adam kept a vigil by his mother's bedside. He held her hand and stared at the face that reminded him so much of Christina. Just the thought of losing both of them made his heart ache.

"Mum, you stay with me, you hear? You're not going anywhere." Sighing, he sat back in the chair, keeping a firm, but gentle grip on her hand. He wished his father could have been there. He was away on a business trip, and although Adam had phoned him, he was unable to get a flight back until the morning.

Worn out and filled with sadness, Adam leaned forward and kissed his mother on the forehead before falling asleep in the uncomfortable chair.

* * *

"Hey! Don't peek. Keep your eyes closed."

Christina giggled. "They're closed!"

Adam took away his hand to reveal the birthday present he'd bought for his sister's seventeenth.

Christina squealed then threw her arms around Adam. "A car!" she screamed. "I can't believe you bought me a car!" She ran over to it and ran her hands lovingly over the bonnet. "It's beautiful!"

Adam smiled. "You have to learn how to drive it first." he chuckled.

"I can't wait!" Christina ran back to her brother and engulfed him in another bear hug.

"You're going away?" Christina's eyes filled with tears. "For how long?"

Adam smiled gently. "Hey, I'm not going far, just to the City. You can come visit me anytime, okay?"

Christina nodded.

"Chrissy? How are you feeling?" Adam asked softly. His heart ached when he saw his sister connected up to a mountain of machinery.

"I'm okay," she whispered. She smiled slightly to try and reassure him.

The monitor next to her beeped monotonously.

Beep. Beep. Beep.

Beeeeeeeeeeeeeeeeeeeeeeeeeeeeeeeeeeeeeeeeeeeep.

* * *

Adam suddenly jolted awake from his dreams. But the continuous beep didn't fade away. Adam looked at the monitor next to him in alarm. The lines were flat. He jumped up and ran to the door.

"Doctor! Nurse! Anybody! Please help my mother!" he shouted down the corridor. The staff were already on their way. They rushed into the room, and a nurse took Adam to wait outside.

"Please," he whispered. "Please don't let her die. I'm begging you. Please." The nurse put her arms around him and held him while he cried.

* * *

Mr Butler ran through the hospital, and was out of breath when he reached the nurses station on the second floor.

"My, my wife," he said breathlessly. "She was brought in yesterday."

The nurse smiled kindly. "And the name, sir?"

"Butler. My wife is Jane Butler."

The nurse flipped through some papers, then bit her lip. She smiled at Mr Butler hesitantly. She stood up. "Could you come with me for a moment please?"

Mr Butler frowned. "Where's my wife? Is she okay? What's happened?"

The nurse took Mr Butler to a small room. Inside, Adam was sitting on the settee, curled up into a little ball.

"Adam!" Mr Butler cried. Adam jumped up and hugged his father. "What's going on? Where's your mother? Is she all right? Why isn't anyone telling me anything?" Mr Butler demanded.

Adam looked up at his father and shook his head. "It doesn't look good, Dad," he said. "She stopped breathing this morning. They got her back, but now she's in a coma in intensive care."

Mr Butler stared at his son. "Oh my God," he whispered. Tears fell freely down his cheeks. He sat down suddenly on the settee, and held his head in his hands. Adam sat next to him.

The nurse standing in the doorway cleared her throat. Mr Butler and Adam looked up.

"Do you want me to leave?" she asked.

"No," Mr Butler said gruffly. "I want you to take me to my wife."

* * *

"Adam? What's happened? I've been trying to get hold of you, where are you?" Melanie's concerned voice filtered through the receiver of the telephone Adam held.

"I'm at the hospital," Adam said quietly. He could hear Melanie gasp.

"What? What's wrong?"

"My, my mum, she, she tried to-" he broke off and started crying for what seemed like the hundredth time that day.

"Stay right where you are, I'll be there as soon as I can," Melanie said. Adam just nodded then hung up the phone.

His dad was by his mother's bedside when he returned to the intensive care unit. Adam put a hand on his hunched shoulder.

"Dad," he said softly. "Go get something to eat. You must be starving."

Mr Butler shook his head miserably. "No, I'm fine."

Adam sighed then took his place on the other side of the bed. He stared at his mother's pale face. She looked just like Christina had when she was ill in hospital. All wired up and full of plastic tubes. There was even a machine helping her to breathe.

'Oh, Christina,' Adam thought sadly. 'If only you didn't have to go, then none of this would ever have happened.'

Later on, Melanie arrived at the intensive care unit. She was shocked when Adam explained to her what had happened over a strong coffee in the hospital cafeteria.

"Adam, I am so sorry. I wish there was something I could do."

Adam shook his head, and stared at the formica table top. "I knew she missed Chrissy, I just didn't realise how much," he said miserably. "I only wish that there was some way Mum could see that Chrissy's in a better place."

Silence fell, Melanie was thinking hard.

"Did you ever check your e-mail?"

"What is it with my e-mail? Why is it so important?" Adam snapped. "My mother's dying in there!"

Melanie winced. "Adam, please. Calm down, it's just... look, the other day, I received an e-mail." She paused and looked Adam in the eye. “From your sister.”

Adam frowned. “But she hadn’t been near a computer in ages.”

Melanie bit her lip. “It was sent the day of her funeral.”

Adam’s eyes widened. “But that’s impossible.”

Melanie smiled. “Apparently not. I thought it was a joke at first, but it was from her, Adam, I’m certain it was. Some of the things she said…” She shook her head. “They were things that only she and I knew about.”

Adam frowned, unwilling to believe. “Really?” He thought for a moment. “And you think she sent me an e-mail too?”

“I’m almost definite that she would have. That’s why I wanted you to check your e-mail. And maybe, if you read it to your mother, she might come around.” Melanie looked at Adam, hoping that she hadn’t upset him.

“My dad’s got his laptop in the car, he carries it everywhere.” Adam looked into Melanie’s eyes. “Do you really think it could work?”

Melanie smiled. “I think it’s worth a try, don’t you?”

Adam nodded. “I’ll try anything.”

Chapter Five

Just minutes later, Melanie and Adam were sat in Mr Butler's car, logging onto the internet through his dad's mobile phone.

The new messages box blinked at them. They looked at each other. Adam took a deep breath and opened his inbox. There were ten new messages.

Melanie pointed to one of them immediately. "That's it," she said. "I recognise the address."

Adam gave a small smile when he read it, it sounded like something his sister would think up.

He opened the e-mail and took a deep breath. By the time he'd finished reading it, he was so shocked all he could do was sit in stunned silence.

He closed his eyes. "Oh my God," he whispered. "It really is from her." He looked at Melanie, and she nodded.

Their eyes locked, and Adam suddenly had the urge to kiss her. He mentally shook himself, and reminded himself of his mother. Quickly, he unpacked the small portable printer and plugged it into the computer. Then he got some paper out of his dad's briefcase. In silence, they printed the e-mail. Then, after putting everything away and hiding it in the boot, Adam and Melanie entered the hospital, hand in hand.

* * *

"'"...Adam, there is one thing I really want you to do for me. Please tell Mum and Dad that they were the best, and that I wish I could have told them that myself, but I knew they'd just tell me that I was going to be fine and I shouldn't talk like that. But Adam, they really are the best parents anyone could have asked for, and I know that you'll love them twice as much now that I'm gone. I also really want Mum to know that I am in an amazing place now. She'd love it here, no stress or worry, just lots of friendly people and plenty of love. But I don't want to see any of you for many years yet, do you hear me? I want you all to live the life that I never had a chance to. Especially you, Adam. Drop that job in the City, I know how much you hate it. And please, do something about what we talked about all the time, okay? I know it would make you happy. Just whatever you do, don't forget me okay?! I love you all very much.

Take care, lots of love, Crispy. (Remember?!)"'"

Adam finished reading the letter to his mother, and looked at her, hoping to see some change, any change; flickering eyelids, moving lips, but there was nothing.

Melanie, who was sitting next to him, squeezed his hand.

"Just wait," she said quietly.

Mr Butler's eyes were getting heavier and heavier and he started dropping off to sleep. After much persuasion, he finally went to the relative's room to get some rest. Over the next few hours, Adam and Melanie sat watching her, taking turns in sleeping. Adam took his gaze off his mother and looked down at Melanie, who was sound asleep in his arms. She looked so innocent and angelic with her blonde hair framing her face. Adam gently brushed aside a stray lock. "Maybe Christina's right," he whispered. Just as he placed a soft kiss on Melanie's forehead, he saw a movement out of the corner of his eye. He looked up quickly. He was definite that his mother just moved. He sat rigid, staring, then suddenly, Mrs Butler's eyes flickered open.

"Chrissy?" she whispered.

"Mum?" he said hoarsely. "Mum, it's me, Adam." Mrs Butler turned her head slightly toward him. Adam nearly shouted out in joy. He shook Melanie gently. "Mel, she's awake!"

Melanie woke up immediately. "What?" she mumbled.

"Mum's awake!"

Melanie sat up, and Adam leaned over the bed and held his mother's hand.

"Mum, can you hear me?"

Mrs Butler smiled slightly. Adam let out a huge sigh of relief. "You just stay here with Melanie, I'll go get Dad and the doctor, okay? Don't fall asleep again." She smiled again at her son.

Adam all but ran to the nurses' station to tell them she was awake, then he ran to where his dad was sleeping and shook him awake. "Dad! Dad wake up!"

Mr Butler jumped up, rubbing sleep out of his eyes. "What? What's wrong? What's happened?"

"It's Mum, she's-"

Mr Butler didn't wait to hear the rest. He sprinted out of the door and down the corridor to the intensive care unit. Adam followed. They arrived, breathing hard, in time to see Mrs Butler smiling and talking to Melanie. Mr Butler gasped in shock.

"She's awake," Adam finished.

Mr Butler went to his wife. He stroked her face. "Oh God, I love you so much," he whispered, kissing her on the forehead.

Mrs Butler smiled. "I love you too," she whispered.

Adam went over to the bed. He kissed his mother on the cheek. "I'm so glad you're awake, Mum."

Just then, a nurse and doctor came into the room. They needed to do some tests. They ushered everyone out into the hallway.

The three of them stood out in the hall, not knowing what to do. Suddenly, Mr Butler started sobbing. Adam went to him and threw his arms around him.

"Hey, Dad, it's okay now," he said, tears running down his own cheeks. "It's okay, Mum's going to be fine. I promise."

Feeling a little awkward, Melanie started to back away a little to give father and son some space, but Adam beckoned her forward and included her in the hug. They stood there for a few minutes, until Mr Butler's sobs finally quietened. He pulled back a little.

"I'm sorry," he said hoarsely. "I was just so scared."

"I know, Dad," Adam whispered. "I was too."

Mr Butler took a deep breath and smiled shakily at Adam.

"I love you, son."

More tears sprang to Adam's eyes. "I love you too, Dad."

Melanie stepped back as father and son bear-hugged, gripping each other like they'd never let go.

* * *

The door to Mrs Butler's room opened, and the three of

them jumped up out of their seats. They looked at the doctor expectantly, all holding their breath.

"Well," the doctor said, looking at his clipboard. "Mrs Butler is a very lucky woman."

They all sighed in relief.

Adam looked at the doctor, then asked hesitantly. "You mean, my mum's going to be okay?"

"She's going to be just fine," he replied, smiling.

Adam let out a whoop and grabbed Melanie around the waist, swinging her around madly.

Mr Butler smiled at the display. He turned to the doctor. "Can I go and see her now?"

The doctor opened the door and ushered Mr Butler in. "She'll be very tired for the next few days, and will need to get plenty of rest, but she should be able to go home fairly soon."

"Thank you, Doctor."

The doctor nodded and left the room, closing the door quietly behind him.

Out in the corridor, he looked at Adam and Melanie, who were still laughing and whooping. "This is an intensive care unit," he said, a hint of a smile on his lips. "Do you think you could keep it down a little?"

Adam and Melanie were instantly quiet and apologised. The doctor said goodbye and walked down the hall.

They looked at each other and grinned.

"I'm so glad your mum's going to be okay," Melanie said softly.

"Yeah, me too," Adam replied.

Melanie glanced down at their entwined fingers, and smiled. Her watch caught her eye and she grimaced. "Oops, it's almost four am!" She looked up at Adam. "My parents will be wondering where I've got to."

“How did you get here?” Adam asked.

“By bus. Mum and Dad were both at work so I couldn’t have the car. I’ll get a taxi back.”

Adam shook his head. “Don’t be silly. I’ll take you home in my dad’s car.”

“Are you sure? You don’t want to stay here with your mum?”

“Well, Dad’s with her, and now I know she’ll be okay, I don’t mind leaving her for a little bit.”

Melanie smiled gratefully. “Well then, a lift would be great, thanks.”

* * *

By the time they reached Melanie’s house, it was nearing five o’clock. Adam parked outside and switched off the engine.

A deep silence engulfed them, broken only by the occasional twittering of birds outside.

Melanie finally broke the silence. “Thanks for the lift.”

Adam turned in his seat to face her.

“It was the least I could do.” He shook his head. “If it wasn’t for you... Mum might never have...”

“Hey,” Melanie whispered. “Don’t cry. Everything’s fine now, just fine.” She leaned forward and hugged Adam, who struggled to keep his tears from falling.

After a few minutes, Adam took a deep breath and pulled away. He looked into Melanie's eyes.

“Seriously though, if you hadn’t told me to check my e-mail, and read it to my mum, she could still be in a coma right now.” He smiled gratefully. “Thank you.”

Melanie smiled back. “I didn’t do anything really. It was Chris who saved her. Maybe you should thank her instead.”

Adam bit his lip. “Yeah, you’re right. I’ll go visit her

tomorrow."

Melanie nodded. She knew Adam regularly visited Christina's grave, to leave flowers and to talk to her.

Melanie glanced over at her house. Through the curtains, she could see the living room light was still on. She smiled and shook her head. "You'd think after I'd been away at uni for three years on my own they would finally stop waiting up for me."

Adam chuckled. "Do you want me to come in and explain?"

"Nah, they'll understand." She touched Adam's hand. "Are you going to be okay?"

Adam nodded. "I'll be fine."

Melanie reached for the door handle and opened the door. Halfway through climbing out, she turned back to Adam. "I've got to ask, I vaguely remember you calling Christina 'Crispy' when we were younger, but I've forgotten why."

Adam grinned. "I was only four when she was born, and I couldn't pronounce her name, so my mum and dad shortened it to Chrissy, but for some reason whenever I said it, it came out as 'Crispy'. And the name just sort of stuck."

Melanie smiled. "I'll see you soon, yeah?"

"Definitely."

Melanie got out the car and shut the door.

Adam started up the engine, waved goodbye, and drove away.

* * *

Ten minutes later, Adam was pacing restlessly around his parents' home. He went from room to room, not knowing what to do with himself. Finally, he found himself at the door of Chrissy's bedroom. He traced her name on the nameplate stuck to her door. He took a deep breath and went in. It was immaculately tidy inside. He figured his mum had probably cleaned it while his sister was in hospital. Maybe she wanted to make it nice in the hope that at some point, Chrissy would come home. He walked around the room, picking up little trinkets and ornaments, smiling at all her stuffed animals that sat at the foot of her bed. He picked up a framed photograph of Chrissy, standing in front of her new car, grinning madly while lovingly stroking the bright blue bonnet.

Adam sat heavily on the bed, staring sadly at her open, happy face. Suddenly overcome with fatigue, Adam lay down on the bed. Clutching the picture to his chest, Adam fell into a deep sleep.

Chapter Six

Adam awoke the next morning with a smile on his face. He'd had a wonderful dream about Chrissy. She was walking along a beach, looking healthy and carefree. A huge smile on her face as she half-ran, half-skipped toward Adam, her arms open to engulf him in a hug. They embraced, and twirled around in mad circles, laughing.

Then she'd pulled back, and he wanted to tell her how much he loved her, and missed her. But she put her finger on his lips, silencing him.

"I know," she had whispered. The she stood on tiptoes and planted a kiss on his forehead. Smiling, she let him go, and walked backwards a few paces. Then she waved, turned around and walked away.

The dream had been so vivid, so clear, that every detail was imprinted in Adam's mind. He put the picture back on Chrissy's bedside table, sat up and stretched. He looked around her room, full of her collections and treasured possessions.

His gaze came to rest on a corner of paper that was poking out of the drawer in the bedside table. Curious, he opened the drawer a little, then stopped. It felt wrong, invading her privacy this way. When they were younger, he'd found a love letter she had written, and read it. When she found out, she was furious with him, and refused to talk to him for an entire week.

He smiled ruefully. It wasn't like it really mattered whether or not he read her personal papers now. He pulled the drawer open fully, and inside was an envelope, with 'Christina Angela Butler's Will' written in tiny letters on it. Adam was surprised. He hadn't realised Chrissy had written a will. She obviously knew that she wouldn't beat the cancer. He opened the envelope carefully, and took out the single sheet of pink paper.

In her will, Christina had requested that her parents not keep her room as a shrine to her, and they were to empty it, giving her possessions to friends and family. Anything that wasn't wanted was to go to a cancer charity shop.

There was a short list of possessions that she wanted to go to particular people. The main one was her diaries, which she wanted Melanie to have. She had kept her secrets in life, and wanted her to keep them in death too.

In the will were details as to where these items were in her room. Adam smiled. Christina had always been very organised. He finished reading and then folded the paper and put it back in the envelope. He placed it on the bedside table and left the room.

He rang the hospital to check on his mum, and to see if she or his dad wanted him to bring anything when he visited a bit later. Then he rang Melanie, to let her know his mum was doing fine, and to thank her for coming to the hospital the day before. She wanted to go with him later to visit, so he said he'd pick her up at two o'clock.

Adam had a shower and changed his clothes. Then he went into the lounge for the first time since he'd found his mum on the floor. Taking a deep breath, he picked up all the photos of Chrissy, putting them in a neat stack on the coffee table. He got the hoover out and cleaned up all traces of his mum's overdose. He straightened the rest of the room, then took the stack of photos, and put them in Chrissy's room.

When he finished that, he decided to go and visit Chrissy's grave before he picked up Melanie. He put on his jacket, and the pocket bleeped. He pulled his mobile phone out and found he had seven missed calls. Every call was from work. He switched the phone off and left it on the hall table, then he jumped into his dad's car and drove to the cemetery.

* * *

Adam walked slowly between the rows of gravestones, the bright April sunlight almost blinding him. He came to Chrissy's grave and stopped. Even though she'd been gone for a few weeks now, her grave still received fresh flowers. The white marble headstone stood in stark contrast to the brightly coloured bouquets. Adam sat on the damp grass, and righted a plastic vase of flowers that had fallen over.

He sat in silence for a moment, then cleared his throat. "Well, thanks to you, little sister, Mum is going to be just fine. I was worried that I might lose the both of you." He stared at a bright pink gerbera in one of the bouquets. "But you saved her. Your words brought her out of the coma and back to this world, and I'm so thankful for that." He smiled. "And, as always, you were right. I do hate my job in the City, and after the last few weeks, I've come to realise that there is more to life than work and money. I want to be happy." He smiled ruefully. "And yes, you were right about Melanie too." He shrugged. "After all these years you'd think I would have given up and accepted that we were just meant to be friends. But I haven't. I love her, and somehow, I'll tell her."

The thought made his stomach clench in anxiety. “I will tell her,” he said more firmly. He reached out and placed his hand on the gravestone.

“Love you, Crispy. I’ll be back soon, okay?”

He stood up and brushed himself off. Then he walked back to the car.

* * *

Later that afternoon, Adam and Melanie arrived at the hospital to find that Mrs Butler was doing so well she’d been moved to a regular ward. Mr Butler was sat by Mrs Butler’s bedside, talking in low, soothing tones. They both looked up when Adam and Melanie arrived. Mrs Butler’s face broke into a smile when she saw her son. She reached out her hand, and Adam stepped forward and gripped it. He sat next to the bed, and smiled at his mother. He was amazed at how much better she looked already. Her skin had lost the slightly grey pallor it had yesterday, and there was colour in her cheeks.

“Hey, Mum, how are you feeling?”

His mum nodded. “Not bad.” She gripped his hand tighter and sighed deeply. “Adam,” she said hoarsely. “I’m so sorry. What I did was stupid, and I’m so sorry that you had to see me like that. It’s just that, well,” her voice broke. “I miss her.”

Adam squeezed her hand gently and leaned forward to wipe away the stray tear on his mother’s cheek. “I know Mum, I miss her too. But instead of trying to deal with it on your own, you should have talked to us, told us how you felt. We would have understood.”

His mother nodded. “I know that now.” She looked from her son to her husband. “I promise I won’t ever do anything like that ever again."

Adam smiled. "Good."

Mrs Butler looked up and saw Melanie standing at the end of her bed, looking awkward.

"Mel, sweetie, come and sit down," she said, smiling warmly at her daughter's best friend.

Melanie smiled back and came forward to sit next to Adam.

"I believe I have you to thank, Melanie, for bringing me round."

Melanie shrugged shyly. "I'm just glad it worked."

"And of course, I should thank my daughter, too," Mrs Butler added softly.

The three of them waited in silence for her to continue.

Mrs Butler smiled wistfully. "It wasn't just her words that brought me back." She squeezed Adam's hand. "I saw her. She told me that there was no way she would let me join her yet, that it was too soon and I needed to stay here." She looked at her husband. "She told me that I had to stay here to look after you, because you'd be lost without me." A tear glistened on her eyelashes. "I'm so sorry that I tried to leave you," she whispered.

"I'm sorry I didn't see how lost you were. I should have been with you more, I could have helped you," Mr Butler replied gruffly.

Suddenly the curtain was pulled back, making them all jump.

"Oh! I'm sorry everyone, didn't mean to frighten you," the ward nurse said "But it's time Mrs Butler got some rest now."

After much persuasion, the nurse allowed Mr Butler to stay by his wife's side while she slept. Adam and Melanie both planted kisses on Mrs Butler's head then left.

* * *

Out in the corridor, Adam paused, making Melanie stop and turn to face him.

"What is it?" she asked.

"Do you have to go home straight away?"

Melanie shook her head. "Why?"

Adam smiled. "Come on," he said, taking Melanie's arm and leading her to the elevator.

In the car, Adam still refused to tell her what was going on, or where they were going. Thirty minutes later, they parked outside Adam's parents' house. Melanie tried once more to find out what Adam was up to, but to no avail.

They went inside, walked through the dark, silent hallway and up the stairs. At the end of the hall they came to Christina's bedroom door. Adam turned around to see Melanie biting her lip.

"It's okay," he said reassuringly. He opened the door and stepped inside. Melanie followed slowly. Adam crossed the room, and sat on the bed. He picked up the envelope containing Chrissy's will and held it out to Melanie. After a moment, she came forward and took the envelope. She took out the pink slip of paper and read silently. Now and then, she smiled. When she finished, she looked at Adam expectantly.

"Chrissy was pretty adamant that you should have her diaries, so I thought you might like to take them now, just in case my parents can't part with them or something." Adam reached under the bed and pulled out a cardboard box.

Melanie put the paper back in the envelope and placed it on the bedside table. She looked at the box with open curiosity but also worry.

"What's wrong?" Adam asked.

"Well, are you sure it's okay for me to just take them? It won't upset your parents?"

Adam smiled. "Of course it's okay. Chrissy wanted you to have them - if you don't take them, then my mum might read them. And it seems that Chrissy didn't want that to happen." He glanced down at the box, which was sealed tight with almost an entire roll of brown tape. He chuckled. "She obviously had a lot of secrets."

Melanie bent down to pick up the box, but Adam put his hand out to stop her.

"It's okay, I'll carry it to the car. It's pretty heavy."

Melanie straightened up. "Normally, I'd be insulted by that very sexist comment. But as it's you, I'll let that one slide." She grinned to show she was joking. She bent down again and attempted to lift the box. Realising just how heavy it was, she gave up.

She looked at Adam and he raised his eyebrows at her.

"Would you like some help with that?" he asked politely.

Melanie shrugged. "Well, okay, if you're offering."

Adam smiled and effortlessly picked the box off the floor. "I'll go put this in the car." He gestured around the room. "See if there's anything else you'd really like to keep. I'll be back in a minute."

After careful thought, Melanie decided to keep a teddy bear that she had once given Chrissy, a silver ring engraved with Chrissy's initials, the baseball cap from their trip to the water park, and a well-worn copy of 'The Hobbit', Chrissy's favourite book. Clutching these to her chest, Melanie took one last look around the room.

"I'll see you, Chris. Love you." She smiled wistfully. Then she left the room, pulling the door closed behind her.

Downstairs, Adam had put the kettle on.

"You all right?" he asked.

Melanie nodded. "Yeah." She held up the things she had chosen. "Feels wrong to be taking her stuff. Like stealing or something."

"Yeah it is weird," Adam agreed. "But I'm sure she'd have liked you to have something to remember her by."

"I don't need things to make me remember Chris. She was a part of my life for so long, I don't think it'll be possible to forget her."

"True. Very true." Adam pointed to the kettle. "Want a cup of tea before I take you home?"

"Sure." Melanie shrugged. "I don't have to rush home yet."

* * *

After a few minutes of talking, the subject of Adam's job came up.

"Is it true what Chrissy said in the e-mail? That you hate it in the City?" Melanie asked, taking a sip of her tea.

Adam sighed. "Yeah, I do." He stared into his cup. "The money is brilliant, the people are great, but I just feel like I'm going nowhere, you know? I've got as high as I can in my department, and there's nowhere else for me to go."

Melanie frowned thoughtfully. "Do you like living there? Aren't there other well-paid jobs that you would enjoy more?"

Adam frowned. "Well, that's just it- I don't really like the City at all. But I wouldn't be able to make the same kind of money anywhere else."

"Is the money that important? Wouldn't it be better to be happy and earn less?"

"I guess so. I'm just not sure what would make me

happy."

Melanie put her hand over his. "You'll work it out. I know you will."

Adam looked down at her hand, and took a deep breath.

"Mel-" he started.

"Adam-" she said simultaneously.

They both laughed.

"You go first," Adam said, a little relieved.

Melanie pulled her hand away. "I should be heading back. I said I'd be back for dinner."

"Okay," Adam said, getting up and putting his cup by the sink. Melanie followed him.

"What was it you were going to say?" she asked.

Adam shook his head. "Nothing important."

* * *

After dinner that night, Melanie left her parents watching a documentary in the living room, and went to her room. The box of Christina's diaries sat in the middle of the floor. Grabbing a pair of scissors from her desk, Melanie sat on the rug and sliced through the tape. She opened the box, and on top of the diaries was a note addressed to her.

"Hey girl,

Well, enclosed in this box are my deepest, darkest secrets! I hope they don't shock you too much, and even maybe bring a smile to your lips. You kept my secrets while I was alive, I'm so glad that you'll keep them for me now that I've gone.

Enjoy!
Love, Chris."

Melanie smiled and put the note aside. She reached into the box and took out the first diary. It was dated 2004. It was the last one Chrissy had written. Melanie wasn't sure she was ready to read that one yet. She looked up at her bookshelf, and decided to swap some of her books for Christina's diaries. She could put them in order and read them from start to finish. After much reorganising, the diaries were finally in place. Feeling a little tired, Melanie selected the first one, dated 1996, settled on her bed, and began to read.

* * *

Reading the thoughts and feelings of a fourteen-year-old Chrissy was very strange to begin with, but as she read on, memories came flooding back and Melanie remembered the awkwardness of being a teenager. Some of the things they had done made Melanie laugh out loud, other things made her cringe at how naive and young they were then. She got to the summer of 1996, and the first camping trip that Chrissy, Melanie and Adam had gone on, that didn't take place in their back garden. They had pitched their tent in a field, just a few miles away. Melanie remembered it well. Although it was the middle of July, it had been freezing cold, and they'd huddled together for warmth.

Melanie's eyes widened as she read the next paragraph. "...I can't believe that Mel hasn't worked it out yet. It's so obvious that Adam is in love with her that it makes me want to puke sometimes! But Mel is completely oblivious. I keep telling Adam to tell her how he feels, but he's so shy! I think they'd make a cute couple, but if they got together then I'd be a third wheel, which wouldn't be so good."

Melanie chuckled. She had no idea that Adam had a crush

on her when they were younger. She'd always liked him, but had never thought they'd be anything other than friends. Chrissy was right, she had been completely oblivious.

Melanie continued to read until well past midnight. She had got into 1997, and couldn't make herself put it down and go to sleep. There were so many things she hadn't known about her best friend.

Eventually, the words were getting blurry and she could barely keep her eyes open. She put the diary on her bedside table, switched off the light and fell asleep instantly.

* * *

The next day, Melanie didn't have anything planned, so she decided to carry on reading Christina's diaries.

By midday, she had reached 1999, Chrissy was now seventeen, and had started having boyfriends. Melanie remembered the hours they spent gossiping about the latest boys in their lives. She sighed. She missed those girlie chats. They had been so young, so carefree, and so happy. It was a pity they'd had to grow up and lose all that.

* * *

After dinner that night, Melanie again went to her bedroom and continued to read. By now she was hooked. She had reached 2003, and had found more than a couple of references to the fact that Adam liked her. The more she read, the more Melanie was convinced that it hadn't been just a teenage crush. By now, she had also found where Chrissy had been diagnosed with cancer. Melanie hadn't realised just how scared Chrissy had been of dying. She hadn't known about all the nights she had lay in her bed and cried. Chrissy had to leave university to live with her parents while having treatment. She had missed her uni friends, the lectures and the freedom. She saw her room as a prison cell. One that she wasn't ever likely to leave alive. A tear came to Melanie's eye when she read her best friend's feelings of complete despair, hopelessness, pain and anger. She was only twenty-one. She hadn't really lived yet. But there was one glimmer of happiness. She had found James. Whom she believed to be her soulmate. She was glad that she had really fallen in love before she died.

The rest of 2003 was filled with much of the same, with small bursts of hope when the doctors had thought she might go into remission. The most upbeat entries were after she had seen James, or her brother. In these entries, Christina mentioned just how much her brother loved Melanie.

"...I can see it in his eyes. Adam loves Melanie just as much as I love James. It's killing him to be so far from her. I couldn't imagine ever being so far away from James. In fact, I don't know how James will cope if I don't get through this. If our positions were reversed, I wouldn't be able to live without him."

By midnight, her arms aching and her eyelids drooping, Melanie got to the very last entry Christina had written, just a few months before.

"Well, this is it. I'm going into hospital for treatment that the doctors hope will help to lengthen my life a little. But I'm not too hopeful. I can feel it in my heart that I will never again lay in this bed. That I will never write in this diary again, and fall asleep surrounded by my things. Goodbye diary, goodbye room, goodbye life. I'll miss you."

Melanie closed the diary and placed it onto her bedside table. It hurt to think that Chrissy hadn't lived long enough to do all the things she'd wanted to do. Melanie resolved then not to waste another minute of her life doing nothing. Tomorrow, she was going to start living.

* * *

When Melanie woke up at eight o'clock the next morning, her gaze rested on the diary on her bedside table. Her promise to herself came back to her. She ripped her covers off, leapt out of bed and grabbed her clothes, jamming them onto her body. She couldn't wait to get going this morning. She had more energy and motivation then she had ever had in her life. Dressed, she opened her door and bounded down the stairs. After a quick coffee, she grabbed her dad's car keys and raced out of the house. Once in the car, she took a moment to decide where to go first. She decided to go and visit Chrissy. She hadn't been to the cemetery since the funeral. Not wanting to go empty handed, she jumped back out of the car and hastily picked some flowers from her parents' front garden. Then she was off. When she arrived at the cemetery, it took her a few minutes to find Chrissy's grave, she had been so upset during the funeral she hadn't taken much notice of its exact location.

When she finally found it, she swallowed hard, a lump suddenly in her throat. Somehow, coming to see Chrissy's gravestone made her death real. She was never going to see her again. Taking a deep breath, she knelt down on the slightly damp grass next to the gravestone. She carefully placed the flowers on the grave.

"Hey Chrissy," she began, not entirely sure what to say. She glanced around to check that no one was listening. "I read your diaries, and you were right, you did have a lot of secrets you naughty girl. Although I wish you'd felt you could have confided some of them in me. But I'm glad that you decided to entrust me with them when you left. I promise I'll keep them to myself. Well, all of them except for one." She smiled. "Why didn't you tell me about your brother? Or is that why you gave me your diaries? So that I would finally get a clue?" She laughed. "Thinking about it now, I can't believe I never noticed the way he looks at me. You're right, it's more than as friends. I hope you're right about how much he loves me. To experience what you and James had would be amazing."

Melanie looked down at her hand and twisted Chrissy's ring around her finger. "I guess I came here to say thank you. For sharing that with me. And that I hope you don't mind me going after your brother. Because I realised last night that I love him too. He's always been more like a big brother to me than anything, but recently..." She looked up at the gravestone and stared at Chrissy's epitaph 'An Angel sleeps here.' "Recently I've been seeing him differently. I would like to get to know him better. Help him make his life more the way he wants it. I'm not sure how yet, but I want to try." She sighed. "Well, I think I've rambled on enough for one day don't you think? I'm sorry it's taken me so long to visit you here. I promise I'll try to come more often." She stood, and blew a kiss toward the gravestone. "See you, Chris."

Melanie turned around, and found herself looking at a pair of very familiar trainers. She looked up to meet Adam's eyes.

Neither of them spoke for a moment, the only sound was the breeze rustling through the trees.

Melanie stood up and bit her lip. "How long have you been standing there?" she whispered.

"A while," Adam replied.

"Oh."

Another silence fell.

"Did you mean it?" Adam asked quietly.

Melanie looked him straight in the eyes. "I meant every word."

Adam took a few steps forward until they were only inches apart. He lifted his hand to caress Melanie's cheek. She closed her eyes and leaned forward until their lips met. Adam wrapped his arms around her, and she melted into his embrace.

* * *

Later that evening, Melanie and Adam sat in his parents' living room talking. About their lives, about Chrissy, and about how stupid Melanie must have been not to see how much he loved her. Every now and then they stopped talking to kiss, both amazed at how natural it felt. They also planned a homecoming party for Adam's mother. She was being released from hospital the next day, and they wanted to give her a warm welcome home. They decided to keep it low key and only invite a couple of very close friends, and keep the banners and balloons inside the house.

At eleven o'clock, Melanie reluctantly left and went home, after arranging to be back at Adam's house by ten o'clock the next morning to help decorate.

Adam went to bed, but didn't fall asleep for a long time. He just kept replaying the scene in the cemetery over and over in his mind, a smile on his face.

* * *

The celebration the next day went smoothly and Mrs Butler was very happy to be home. She'd had enough of the sterile white of the hospital rooms. She looked much healthier after the rest and care, and Adam was glad to see her looking so cheerful. He felt certain that she would be okay now. That she wouldn't lapse back into such a terrible depression again.

Seeing how his mother was bravely stepping forward in life, Adam decided it was about time he did the same. So he finally rang his boss and told him he would be handing in his resignation. His boss wasn't very happy, but Adam couldn't be persuaded to stay. The following weekend, Adam hired a van, and Melanie went with him to his flat to help him move out.

Fed up with living with her parents, Melanie and Adam decided to find a flat together. It was a huge step to take so quickly, but they both felt it was the right thing to do.

Chapter Seven

A few weeks after moving in with each other, Melanie and Adam were walking through town, on their way to the hardware shop to buy some paint for the bedroom. They were having a very spirited argument over the colour as they walked along. Halfway through a sentence, Melanie looked up and stopped suddenly. Jolted by the sudden halt, Adam looked up and saw what Melanie was looking at.

It was James. He was walking toward them, his hands deep in his pockets, his shoulders hunched over and his head hung low.

Melanie broke away from Adam and walked forward to meet James. He looked up at her, and the deep sadness in his eyes tore her apart.

Without a word, she stepped forward to hug him. He didn't respond at first, but after a moment he put his arms around her and gripped her tight.

After a few minutes they stepped apart. Adam came to stand next to Melanie. She rubbed James' arm.

"How are you doing?" she asked, for lack of something better to say.

James shrugged. He cleared his throat. His voice sounded scratchy, as if he hadn't spoken in a while.

"I'm okay," he said, unconvincingly.

Melanie remembered what Chrissy said in her diary about James being lost without her. It seemed she had been right, as always.

"Is there anything we can do?" she asked him softly.

James looked at his feet and shook his head. "I'll be all right." He looked up at Adam. "I, uh, I heard about your mum. Is she okay?"

Adam nodded. "She's fine, thanks."

James stared back down at his feet. "That's good. I'm glad to hear it."

Melanie put her hand on his shoulder. "Are you sure there's nothing we can do?"

James shook his head again. "I'll be okay."

"Would you like to join us for a coffee or something?"

James glanced at his watch. "I can't right now, I have to get going. It was good to see you guys though."

Adam smiled. "Yeah, take care okay?"

James looked at the two of them, now holding hands, and nodded slightly. "See you around."

* * *

For hours that evening, James sat on the rocks down the beach. He cried silently as he watched the sunset. Every day, when the sun dropped below the horizon, it brought him painful memories of how he hadn't been able to say his final goodbyes to the girl that he loved with all his heart. If only she'd stayed awake until he could have reached her. If only he knew that she was okay.

"Oh, Christina," he whispered, his words whipped away by the wind. "Wasn't my love enough to keep you on this Earth for just a few more minutes?"

Then he thought back to earlier that afternoon. Adam and Melanie looked so happy and so comfortable with each other. Although he'd always known they liked each other - Chrissy had told him - it made his heart ache. It reminded him so much of all the times he and Chrissy had spent together. Not doing anything in particular, just walking around, holding hands. Or sitting on this very beach, talking about their plans for the future. Chrissy's dream had been to be an actress. All she wanted to do was have her name and face splashed all over movie posters. James smiled sadly to himself as he remembered all the films they had rented, and he had lost count long ago of how many times she'd dragged him to the cinema. Her ultimate favourite film, was 'City of Angels'. They'd watched it so many times, James could probably act out the whole thing. He now understood exactly how the guy in the film must have felt when the woman he loved had died.

"Why, Chrissy?" he shouted at the sea. "Why couldn't you have stayed for just a few more minutes?"

But his questions were left unanswered.

As darkness settled like a blanket over him, he dropped his head in his arms and grieved.

* * *

The flat was empty, dark and cold when James arrived home. It was always cold now, without Chrissy. He went to the fridge and took out a beer. He didn't bother with food, lately he just didn't seem to have an appetite. Slowly he trudged into his bedroom, not bothering to turn on the light. As his eyes adjusted to the dark, a framed photo of Christina and himself came into view. He sighed. Even his bedroom reminded him of her. They'd spent hours here, talking, laughing, tickling each other or just having long conversations over coffee. He set the beer on his bedside table, then lay on his bed, staring at the ceiling. The silence of the flat was overwhelming. James wished then that he'd taken Melanie up on her offer. All he wanted right then was some company. But he knew he didn't want just any company. He wanted Chrissy. He wanted her back so badly that he could barely stand the pain of her not being there with him. A huge black void had swallowed her, and James was in danger of being swallowed by it too. James sat up and opened his bedside table drawer. He took out the weathered, battered old wooden box that lay within it. He sat with it on his lap for a long time. Just as he had done almost every evening since Chrissy had left him. He stared at it in the falling darkness. He knew, that inside, was a solution. A solution to all of his problems, his sadness, grief and deep depression. If he chose to open the box to solve his problems, he would be with her again. He could join her in the next world. Just the thought of seeing her again brought a smile to his chapped lips.

He sighed, caressed the box, then, like he did every evening, he put the box back in the drawer, and resolved to not do that again. But he knew he would. And one day, he might even choose the easy way out. It wasn't that he wanted to die. It was just that he couldn't bear to live without Chrissy. His world without her was grey, hopeless, a void in which to drown in.

Slowly, James came out of his reverie and looked around his room. He was searching for a diversion from the black void that was trying to engulf him.

His gaze settled on his computer. He hadn't been on the internet since he'd sent the e-mails for Christina. He stood up and went over to his desk. Minutes later, he was logging onto the internet. He didn't bother to check his e-mail, instead, he went to a chat room. But none of the conversations really held his interest, so he exited there and checked his e-mail instead. He had twenty-three messages. James read through them. "Junk," he muttered, "junk, junk and more junk." He went through them again, this time, deleting them. But suddenly, one of the junk mail subjects caught his eye. Frowning, he clicked on it to open it. Had he not been sitting down, the first few words of the e-mail would have made him fall over.

"This is impossible," he muttered to the screen. "What the...?" Slowly, he read through the whole e-mail, his eyes getting wider with each word.

"Dear James,

I know you are not going to believe this e-mail is real, but it really is from me, your angel, Chrissy. Thank you so much for sending those e-mails to everyone. When I saw just how much they helped everyone, especially my mother, I realised then that I had to send you one last one, in the hope it would help you too.

There's something you need to know, James. Do you remember the dream I told you about? About the two of us walking along the beach? That's where I am. In the warm sunshine, free of pain, with all my memories of you to keep me company.

I know what you've been thinking, and I am begging you not to do it. It's too early for you to join me, James. I'll be here waiting for you when the time comes, but that won't be for a long time.

I want you to be happy. I want you to live the life that I couldn't. To realise your dreams and live them. Please don't spend the rest of your life crying for me at sunset and praying for my forgiveness. There is nothing to forgive. My only regret is *not* that you arrived too late, but that I made you feel so guilty for arriving too late. I shouldn't have tried to force you to do something you didn't want to do. So I hope that you forgive me for that.

On a lighter note, I'm so glad that Melanie and Adam finally got together - I told you they would, didn't I? Oh, and could you please apologise to Peter? You know he was my friend long before you and I met, and that he loved me too. There was no need to hit him.

Well, I think it's time for me to go now. I just wanted you to know that this is not the end. I'm still here. I'm still watching you. And you are still there. You need to keep breathing, living, laughing, loving. Don't forget me, but don't let the memory of me take over your life either.

I'll see you on the beach,
Love for eternity,
Your angel, Chrissy."

* * *

The sky was all different shades of pink, purple and orange when James arrived at the beach. There wasn't a single breath of wind. James stood on a rock, at the edge of the cliff, looking down at the waves lapping the shore. The sun was falling quickly toward the horizon. James stood quietly, listening to the sounds that surrounded him. Then as the sun met the horizon, instead of crying, James smiled.

"Thank you, Chrissy. I won't cry anymore," he said, reaching into his pocket. "I've made my decision, and I know it's the right one." He lifted up the gun. The late evening sun glinted on it as it moved. "You're my soulmate,

Chrissy. There will never be anyone else that I could love as much as I love you."

He stared down at the gun in his hand. "But that doesn't mean I should give up. I'm sorry that I considered it. I just wanted to see you again so badly."

He took a deep breath. Then he pulled his arm back and threw the gun as hard as he could into the calm water below.

He raised the white rose in his other hand to his lips and kissed it gently.

"Goodbye, Chrissy," he whispered. "Goodbye, my Angel."

Then he threw the rose into the sea. He watched it for a few moments, as it got carried away by the gentle waves. Then he turned from the edge, and walked away.

About the Author

Michelle lives in the UK, when she's not flitting in and out of other realms. She believes in Faeries and Unicorns and thinks the world needs more magic and fun in it. She writes because she would go crazy if she didn't. She might already be a little crazy, so please buy more books so she can keep writing.

Please feel free to write a review of this book. Michelle loves to get direct feedback, so if you would like to contact her, please e-mail theamethystangel@hotmail.co.uk or keep up to date by following her blog – **TwinFlameBlog.com.** You can also follow her on Twitter **@themiraclemuse** or like her page on Facebook.

You can now become an Earth Angel Trainee:
earthangelacademy.co.uk

To sign up to her mailing list, visit:
michellegordon.co.uk

Where's My F**king Unicorn?

Are your bookshelves filled with self-help books, and yet your life feels empty? Do you keep following paths to enlightenment that lead to the same dead ends? You've read the books, attended the seminars and taken heed of every bit of advice going... but you're still waiting for your f**king unicorn to come along! Where's My F**king Unicorn? is a guide to life, creativity and happiness that offers a very different way forward. Author, Michelle Gordon, explains why, in spite of all your best efforts, your life still doesn't live up to your vision of what it should be, and tells you exactly what you can do about it. In refreshingly down-to-earth language, she shows you how to harness all the self-knowledge you have gained from all those self-help books you've read, and actually start putting it to practical use.

Earth Angel Series:

The Earth Angel Training Academy (book 1)

There are humans on Earth, who are not, in fact, human.
They are **Earth Angels**.
Earth Angels are beings who have come from other realms, dimensions and planets, and are choosing to be born on Earth in human form for just **one** reason.
To **Awaken the world**.
Before they can carry out their perilous mission, they must first learn how to be human.
The best place they can do that, is at
The Earth Angel Training Academy

The Earth Angel Awakening (book 2)

After learning how to be human at the Earth Angel Training Academy, the Angels, Faeries, Merpeople and Starpeople are born into human bodies on Earth.
Their Mission? **Awaken the world**.
But even though they **chose** to go to Earth, and they chose to be human, it doesn't mean that it will be **easy** for them to Awaken themselves.
Only if they **reconnect** to their **origins**,
and to other Earth Angels, will they will be able to
remember who they really are.
Only then, will they experience
The Earth Angel Awakening

The Other Side (book 3)

There is an Angel who holds the world in her hands.

She is the **Angel of Destiny**.

Her actions will start the **ripples** that will **save humans** from their certain demise.

In order for her to initiate the necessary changes, she must travel to other **galaxies**, and call upon the most **enlightened** and **evolved** beings of the Universe.

To save **humankind**.

When they agree, she wishes to prepare them for Earth life, and so invites them to attend the Earth Angel Training Academy, on

The Other Side

The Twin Flame Reunion (book 4)

The Earth Angels' missions are clear: **Awaken** the world, and move humanity into the **Golden Age**.

But there is another reason many of the Earth Angels choose to come to Earth.

To **reunite** with their **Twin Flames**.

The Twin Flame connection is deep, everlasting and intense, and happens only at the **end of an age**. Many Flames have not been together for millennia, some have never met.

Once on Earth, every Earth Angel longs to meet their Flame.

The one who will make them **feel at home**, who will make living on this planet bearable.

But no one knows if they will actually get to experience

The Twin Flame Reunion

The Twin Flame Retreat (book 5)

The question in the minds of many Earth Angels
on Earth right now is:
Where is my **Twin Flame?**
Though many Earth Angels are now meeting their Flames,
the circumstances around their reunion can have
life-altering consequences.
If meeting your Flame meant your life would never be the
same again, would you still want to find them?
When in need of **support** and answers,
Earth Angels attend
The Twin Flame Retreat

The Twin Flame Resurrection (book 6)

Twin Flames are **destined** to meet. And when they are
meant to be together, nothing can keep them apart.
Not even **death**.
When Earth Angels go home to the Fifth Dimension too
soon, they have the **choice** to come back.
To be with their **Twin Flame**.
The connection can be so overwhelming, that some Earth
Angels try to resist it, try to push it away.
But it is **undeniable**.
When things don't go according to plan, the universe steps in,
and the Earth Angels experience
The Twin Flame Ressurrection

The Twin Flame Reality (book 7)

Being an Earth Angel on Earth can be difficult, especially when it doesn't feel like home, and when there's a deep longing for a realm or dimension where you feel you **belong**.

Finding a Twin Flame, is like **coming home**.

Losing one, can be **devastating**.

Adrift, lonely, isolated... an Earth Angel would be forgiven for preferring to go home, than to stay here **without their Flame**.

But if they can find the **strength** to stay, to follow their mission to **Awaken** the world, and fulfil their original purpose, they will find they can be **happy** here.

Even despite the sadness of

The Twin Flame Reality

The Twin Flame Rebellion (book 8)

The Angels on the Other Side have a **duty** to **help** their human charges, but **only** when they are **asked** for help.

They are not allowed to meddle with **Free Will**.

But a number of Angels are asked to break their **Golden Rule**, and start influencing the human lives of the Earth Angels.

Once the Angels start nudging, they find they can't stop, and when the Earth Angels find out they are being manipulated from the Other Side, they aren't happy.

Determined to **choose** their own **fate**,

the Earth Angels embark on

The Twin Flame Rebellion

The Twin Flame Reignition (book 9)

The **destiny** of many **Twin Flames** is changing. Those destined to remain apart on Earth are hearing the call to come **together.**

As things begin to shift and change, it suddenly it seems **possible** for them to **reunite,** and have the lives they always **dreamed** of.

But when **visions** and **dreams** of **Atlantis** begin to plague the Earth Angels, and they try to work out their meaning, what they **discover** may jeopardise

The Twin Flame Reignition

The Earth Angel Revolution (book 10)

When a Seer has a **vision** of the **Golden Age**, she takes drastic action in order to make it happen.

The consequences of her actions are so **epic** that the lives of every **Earth Angel** and every **human** on Earth will be altered **forever.**

She enlists the help of two **Angels** to assist her in

The Earth Angel Revolution

Visionary Collection:

Heaven dot com

When Christina goes into hospital for the final time, and knows that she is about to lose her battle with cancer, she asks her boyfriend, James, to help her deliver messages to her family and friends after she has gone.

She also asks him to do something for her, but she dies before he can make it happen, and he finds it difficult to forgive himself.

After her death, her messages are received by her loved ones, and the impact her words have will change their lives forever.

The Doorway to P.A.M

Natalie is an ordinary girl who has lost her way. There is nothing particularly special about her or her life. She has no exceptional abilities. She hasn't achieved anything miraculous. Her life has very little meaning to it.

Evelyn is the caretaker at Pam's. The alternate dimension where souls at their lowest point find the answers they need to turn their lives around. The dimension dreamers visit, to help people while they sleep.

One ordinary girl, one extraordinary woman.
One fated meeting that will change lives.

The Elphite

Ellie's life is just one long, bad case of déjà vu. She has lived her life before - a hundred times before - and she remembers each and every lifetime.
Each time, she has changed things, but has never managed to change the ending.
This time, in this life, she hopes that it will be different.
So she makes the biggest change of all - she tries to avoid meeting him.
Her soulmate. The love of her life.
Because maybe if they don't meet, she can finally change her destiny.
But fate has other ideas...

I'm Here

When Marielle finds out that a guy she had a crush on in school has passed away, the strange occurrences of the previous week begin to make sense. She suspects that he is trying to give her a message from the other side, and so opens up to communicate with him, She has no idea that by doing so, she will be forming a bond so strong, that life as she knows it will forever be changed.

Nathan assumed that when he died, he would move on, and continue his spiritual journey. But instead he finds himself drawn to a girl that he once knew. The more he watches her, and gets to know her, he realises that he was drawn to her for a reason, and that once he knows what that is, he will be able to change his destiny.

The Onist

Valerie is just a typical sixteen year old girl, until the moment that her consciousness slips into the body of another woman and causes a car crash.

She thinks it was just a vivid daydream until she finds a news article confirming the death of a woman the night before.

When Valerie begins to shift into the minds of other women, she finds herself in a dangerous situation, and must find a way to stop it before she becomes lost.

Duelling Poets

For 30 days in 2012, Michelle and Victor wrote a poem a day, taking turns to choose the titles.

Michelle is an author, who was in her late 20s at the time, and Victor a retired journalist in his 70s. Their differing experiences and perspectives created contrasting poems, despite being written about the same topic.

In Duelling Poets, we invite you to read the poems and choose your favourites, then at the end, you can see which poet wins the duel for you.

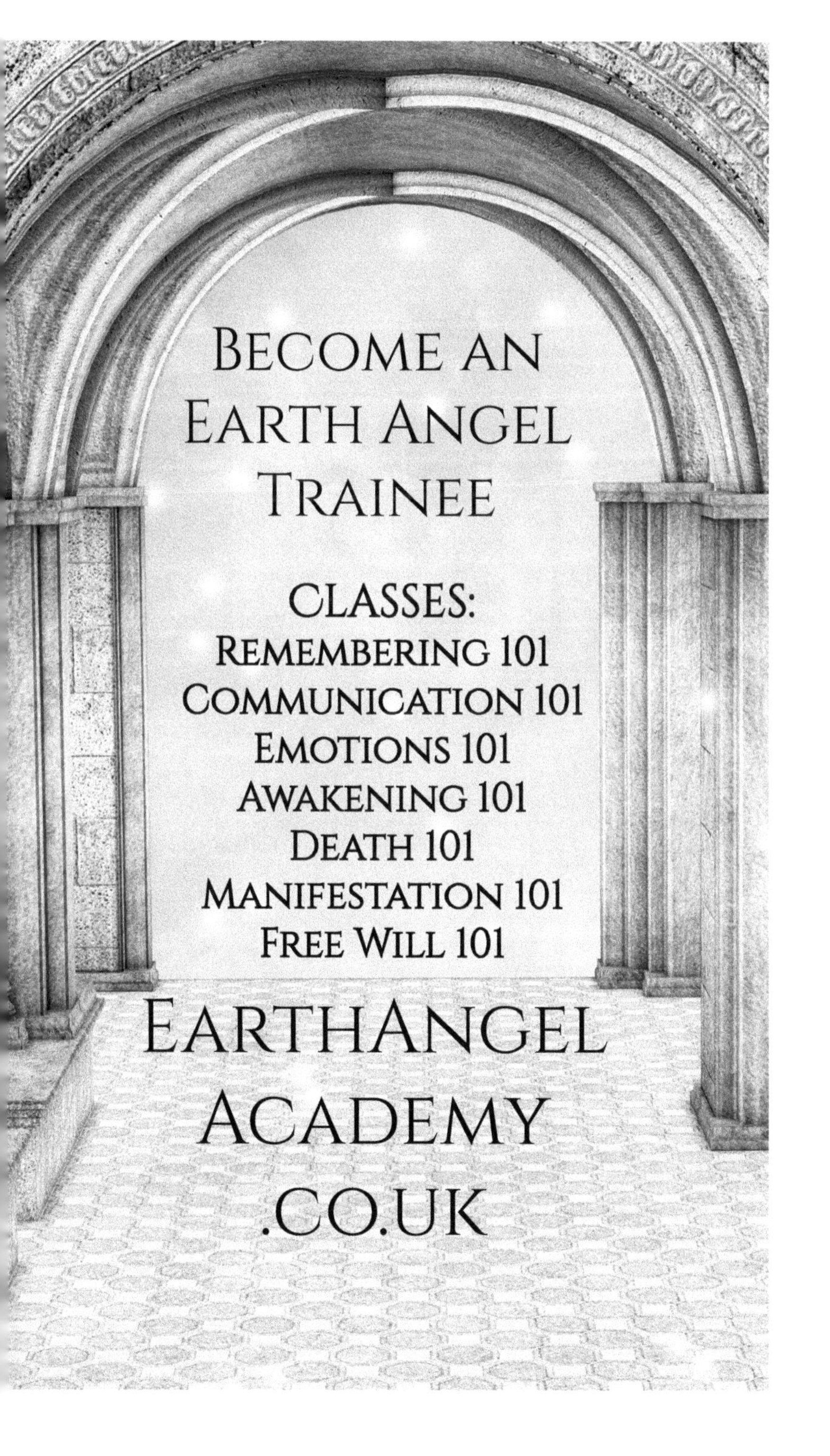

Lightning Source UK Ltd.
Milton Keynes UK
UKHW02f0625220518
323007UK00012B/834/P

9 781912 257300